The Witch's Children

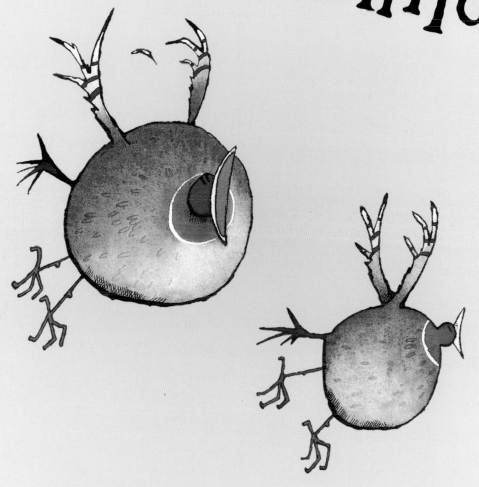

ORCHARD BOOKS

96 Leonard Street

London EC2A 4XD

Orchard Books Australia

32/45-51 Huntley Street, Alexandria, NSW 2015

ISBN 1 84121 551 1 (hardback)

ISBN 1 84121 114 1 (paperback)

First published in Great Britain in 2001

First paperback edition in 2002

A CIP catalogue record for this book is available
from the British Library.

10 9 8 7 6 5 4 3 2 (hardback)

10 9 8 7 6 5 (paperback)

Printed in China

The Witch's Children

Written by

Ursula Jones

Illustrated by

Russell Ayto

ORCHARD BOOKS

for Charlotte
U.J.

for Matthew and Daniel
R.A.

One windy day the witch's children went to the park.

"Look out," said the pigeons,
"here come the witch's children!"
And they flew into the trees.

"Look out," said the squirrels,
"the witch's children are coming
and that means TROUBLE!"
And they ran up the tree trunks
into the wind tossed trees.

It was quite crowded up there.

The witch's children bought ice creams
from the ice cream lady.
The Eldest and the Middle One bought two each.
The Little One bought three.

"So far, no trouble," said the pigeons to the squirrels.

The witch's children came to the pond.
Gemma was sailing her boat.

The wind blew

and blew.

*It blew the
boat over.*

"Oh, no!" shouted Gemma. "Who will save my little boat from sinking?"

"I will," said the Eldest One and he changed Gemma ...

... into ...

... a frog.

"Swim out and rescue your boat," said the
Eldest One to the frog. So Gemma did.

"That was fun," said Gemma.
"Change me back now please."
"Can't," said the Eldest One.
"I haven't learned how to do that yet."
The frog cried and cried.
"Now we've got trouble,"
cooed the pigeons.

And the Little One
laughed till she
fell over.

"Don't worry, Gemma,"
said the Middle One to
the frog. "Watch."

She changed the trees
into a huge palace.

And the
pigeons into
fat footmen.

And the squirrels
into smart soldiers.

She changed the ice cream
van into a golden coach.

And the ice
cream lady into
a fair princess.

"Kiss the frog,"
said the witch's child
to the princess.

So the princess did.

And the frog turned
into a handsome prince.

"That's no good," said the prince.
"I want to be Gemma. Change us all back."

"Yes," snapped the princess, "this coach is full of melted ice cream. Change us back."

"Can't," said the Middle One. "I haven't learned how to do that yet."

"Now we're in trouble," sighed the footmen to the soldiers.

And the Little One laughed till she split her trousers.

"STOP THAT!"

they all shouted. "And get us out of trouble."
The Little One felt sorry she'd laughed at them.
"I only know one bit of magic."

"Well, try it!"

they all said.
The Little One opened her mouth
wide and yelled...

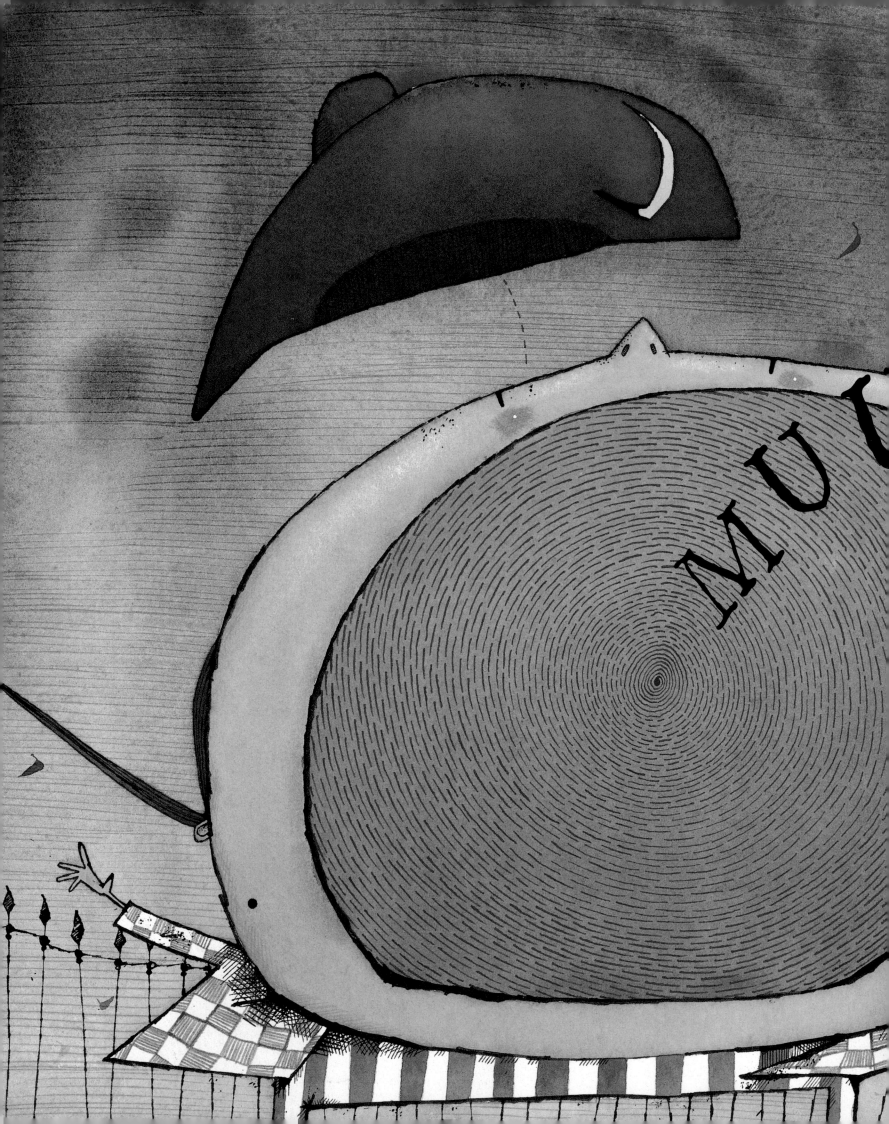

And...

WHOOSH!

Out of the clouds flew the
witch on her broomstick.

She changed the handsome prince back into Gemma...

the fair princess back into the ice cream lady...

the golden coach back into the ice cream van...

the smart soldiers back
into the squirrels...

the fat footmen
back into the
pigeons...

and the huge palace
back into the trees.

And they
were all happy.

Especially the Little One.